Brady Brady
and the Great Rink

Written by Mary Shaw
Illustrated by Chuck Temple

PUBLISHED BY
BRADY BRADY INC.

Published in Canada in 2004 by

Brady Brady Inc.
P.O. Box 367
Waterloo, Ontario
Canada
N2J 4A4

Canadian Cataloguing in Publication Data

ISBN 0-9735557-0-X

Brady joins his first hockey team and builds a backyard skating rink.
Introduction to the Brady Brady series.

Printed and bound in Canada

Keep adding to your Brady Brady book collection. Make sure you read:

- **Brady Brady and the Super Skater**
- **Brady Brady and the Runaway Goalie**
- **Brady Brady and the Twirlin' Torpedo**
- **Brady Brady and the Singing Tree**
- **Brady Brady and the Big Mistake**
- **Brady Brady and the Great Exchange**
- **Brady Brady and the Most Important Game**
- **Brady Brady and the MVP**

To my own Brady Brady
Mary Shaw

Dedicated to the memory of my proud, loving father,
Chuck Sr — who was always there for me
Chuck Temple Jr.

Brady loved winter. He loved winter because he loved to skate.
He loved to skate because he loved hockey.
Hockey was all Brady thought about.

It drove his family **_crrraaazy!_**
They had to call him twice
to get his attention.

"Brady, Brady!
Stop thinking about hockey.
Eat your potatoes."

"Brady, Brady! Brush your teeth."

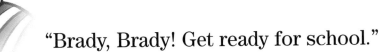

"Brady, Brady! Get ready for school."

"Brady, Brady! Don't forget your lunch."

Everyone got so used to calling him
twice that they simply named
him Brady Brady.

It was easier that way.

Brady was on a team called the Icehogs.
When hockey season arrived and the Icehogs started to play,
Brady thought less about everything else
and even more about hockey.

When Brady wasn't playing hockey, he was "snow-watching." Every morning he leapt out of bed to see if a storm had dumped snow in his backyard. Back in the summer he had decided that when the snow came, he would build something incredible! One Saturday morning it finally happened. The backyard was covered in snow.

"Whoo-hoo!" he shouted, shaking the dog's basket. "Come on, Hatrick! We've got work to do."

"Slow down, pal," his dad chuckled, as Brady gobbled down his cereal. "Where's the fire?"

"No fire, Dad. Just snow. Lots of it!" Climbing up onto his chair, Brady announced, "Today I am going to build the greatest backyard rink ever! Kids will come from all over town to play hockey on it."

"You're crazy. It's too much work," said his sister.

"Brady Brady, your nose will freeze off," warned his mom.

"I'd help, but I'm allergic to the cold," muttered his dad.

"That's okay. I can do it myself," Brady boasted as he bundled up in his snowsuit, boots, and hat. His mom helped with the mittens — two pairs, to stay extra warm.

Brady shuffled his feet in the snow
and made the outline of his rink.
It was as big as the whole backyard.

With his dad's big shovel,
Brady heaved snow
over to the sides.

Snowbanks grew higher and higher, but not quite high
enough to block the sight of his sister drinking hot chocolate
in the warm kitchen.

Brady could hardly lift the sandwich his mother brought out
for lunch. As he pounded down the snow to make
his rink smooth, Brady was certain it was
his arms — not his nose — that would fall off.

It was almost dark when Brady finished his pounding.
He took a squirt bottle full of raspberry juice and drew a
red face-off circle. With a squirt bottle of blueberry juice he
drew two blue lines, just like on a real hockey rink. He dragged
the hose out and began flooding his rink. The water froze.
Brady almost froze along with it.

That night he collapsed into bed, barely able to move. "See,
Mom?" he sniffed. "My nose didn't fall off."

In the morning, Brady woke up to find his rink buried in snow.

"I told you it was too much work," said his sister.

"Brady Brady, you'll turn into a snowman," warned his mom.

"Too bad I have such a bad back," muttered his dad.

After shoveling for hours, Brady flooded his rink. When Hatrick chased a squirrel across it, he flooded the rink once more.

Again, he fell into bed at night, barely able to give his mom a hug.

On snowy days Brady shoveled his rink.

On really cold days he flooded his rink.

And every day, no matter how
tired or cold he was,
Brady skated on his rink.

"The rink is too bumpy," said his sister.

"You'll wear yourself out," warned his mom.

"I can't find my skates," muttered his dad.

Brady would skate for hours.
He practiced his crossovers, backwards skating, and stopping.
Sometimes Hatrick helped by standing in net
while Brady perfected his shot.

Brady's skating got better and better.
And just in time. Tomorrow the Icehogs
were playing in their biggest game yet — the Frosty Cup.

That night Brady was so excited, he slept in his equipment.

Brady was the first to arrive in the dressing room.
He high-fived his teammates as they came in,
hoping they were as pumped up about the game as he was.

When everyone had their uniforms on and skates laced up,
they huddled in the center of the room and began their team cheer.

"We've got the power,
We've got the might,
We've got the spirit . . .

They waited and waited. Finally the coach spoke up. "Looks like the power is out in the whole building. I'm afraid we can't play for the Frosty Cup after all. Everyone take off your equipment."

Brady didn't need any lights on to know what his teammates looked like. He could hear the moans and groans as they started to unlace their skates in the dark. They were as heartbroken as he was.

*"**Wait!**"* cried Brady. "I know a ***great*** rink where we can play."

It was the coolest hockey game ever played.
People came from all over town.

It was so much fun that nobody even cared about the score!

And when Brady saw the happy faces around him, he knew he truly had built the greatest backyard rink *ever!*